THE BROKEN
FANG

BY

UEL KEY

British Library Cataloguing-in-Publication Data
A catalogue record for this book is available from the
British Library

CONTENTS

UEL KEY

Uel Key was the pseudonym of Samuel Whittell Key, born in 1874. Key wrote a number of short stories, all of which have Professor Arnold Rhymer, an occult detective and doctor, as their protagonist. Rhymer has a deductive mind and sharp wit, and is widely regarded as something of an homage to Arthur Conan Doyle's Sherlock Holmes. Key's stories all appeared in the prestigious *Pearson's Magazine* in 1917 and 1918 and were later anthologised in *The Broken Fang and Other Experiences of a Specialist in Spooks*, published in 1920. A year later, Key produced a novel, also starring Prof. Arnold Rhymer, entitled *The Yellow Death*. Key died aged 74.

THE BROKEN FANG

UEL KEY

'Sorry to trouble you, sir, but can you help to clear up a mystery which, I'm bound to own, is baffling us?'

The individual thus addressing Professor Arnold Rhymer, MD – the young and distinguished *savant* in psychical phenomena – was a big, finely-built man. He placed his hat and stick on the table and deposited his frame in an easy chair, to which the professor motioned him.

'My name is Brown,' he explained, 'Detective-Inspector Brown of the CID, Scotland Yard. My chief has put me on to a case which doesn't seem quite – well – normal, you know. These sort of problems are in your line, I believe; or else I shouldn't have bothered you.'

'What's the nature of your case?'

'The Blankborough murders. Surely you've read about these mysterious crimes committed near the country town of Blankborough?'

'Yes,' Rhymer admitted, 'but the papers don't give much

3

detail.'

'I know, for we've suppressed details to disarm the criminal, until we've got hold of some sort of clue towards identification. That'll be no easy matter, though, I dare bet. Will you help us, sir?'

'I'll give you what assistance I can,' he replied, 'but I shall want some details first, for I know nothing more than the newspapers have outlined, and, as you admit, that amounts to very little.'

'I'll be frank with you,' the detective affirmed; 'but what I've to tell you is confidential.'

'I shan't say a word.'

'The police-surgeon,' Brown continued, 'laid emphasis upon two points of deduction. The first was that he did not believe – judging from the appearance of the corpses – that the victims had succumbed as a direct result of the mutilated condition of the bodies.'

'That was certainly the impression I gathered from the reports,' Rhymer volunteered. 'Three healthy young men murdered in one week, in the same locality – close to a peaceful country town, and their bodies mutilated with some sharp instrument.'

'Just so,' Brown acquiesced, 'only the surgeon held a different opinion, since he discovered two punctures in the neck of each victim, and he was convinced that death was primarily due to a loss of blood from these incisions. His second deduction was that these wounds were inflicted with something sharp and wedge-shaped, and that the identically same thing was not used in wounding the third victim – or possibly the first – since the end was found broken off and embedded in the neck of the second victim.'

Rhymer seemed puzzled as he mentally absorbed these details.

'Were the wounds in the necks small?' he queried.

'Quite.'

'Merely incisions, not gashes?'

'Yes.'

'Then it seems improbable that the victims rapidly bled to death from these wounds alone?'

'That's what struck me at the time; but I've yet to add that the surgeon's opinion was that death supervened in each case from haemorrhage, probably due to suction, as though a small vacuum pump had been applied to the incisions.'

'Or the mouth of some living creature?' Rhymer hazarded with a significant glance.

'Good heavens! that never occurred to me,' the detective cried.

Rhymer pursed his lips and his brow contracted as he asked:

'What was the broken piece like, found in the wound of

victim number two?'

For reply, Brown searched his waistcoat pockets and produced a small metal box. This he opened and handed to Rhymer.

The latter took it and, glancing within, suddenly stifled an exclamation, for that which he beheld revealed a supposition more horrible than he had previously contemplated.

'Don't mislay that piece of evidence, whatever you do,' he enjoined, handing the box back to the detective. 'This is going to prove a complicated case,' he added, 'but it'll furnish us with interest and excitement as well, I'll be bound.'

'I guessed it would be in your line, sir, for I've heard tell that you're OK on abnormal problems, and this one's creepy enough for anything.'

Later on in the day Professor Rhymer left his flat in Whitehall Court and, meeting Inspector Brown, by arrangement, at Charing Cross station, they boarded an evening train for Blankborough, arriving there an hour later. They at once proceeded to the best of the several inns which the little town afforded. This house – quite a superior hostelry of its kind – was known as the King's Arms Hotel. Brown had previously taken up his quarters there when recently visiting the scene of the murders. After a frugal war-meal, Rhymer proposed a quiet stroll, where they might be free from interruption or chance eavesdroppers. Accordingly they sauntered out into the old-fashioned town – the detective leading his companion along several back streets and alleys, which eventually brought them into a lonely country lane.

'Now we are free to talk without much fear of being overheard,' Rhymer remarked, 'and there are several things I want to ask you.'

'Fire away, then, sir.'

'I take it you've viewed the bodies of the victims.'

'Yes,' replied Brown, 'I saw them yesterday.'

'Did you happen to notice if each body was mutilated in a similar manner?'

'I noticed that the mutilations were alike in this respect – the bodies appeared to have been ruthlessly hacked about with a keen-bladed weapon of sorts. It resembled the work of a fanatic more than a responsible person.'

'So the police-surgeon thought these poor fellows weren't killed by violence as their remains seemed to suggest?'

'He intimated as much.'

'Then how on earth did he account for their mangled condition?'

'Oh, he put that down to the assassin's endeavour to create a false impression, that its victims had been killed in that way; or possibly to lessen the chance of identification. He was, however, inclined to favour the former theory, since the corpses were not so badly disfigured as to cause any difficulty in the latter direction.'

'Were the victims robbed?'

'No; they were all respectable young fellows, of the artisan type, who don't usually carry valuables about; but their pockets, containing some treasury notes and loose silver – being pay day – were intact. A solid gold watch was discovered on one of the bodies – evidently a presentation, from the inscription it contained. So robbery is entirely out of the question.'

'One thing's very evident,' Rhymer remarked, 'these murders were not committed by an ordinary individual. They're not a bit like common crimes done for revenge or robbery: there's evidently a far deeper motive than external appearances present.'

'Not unlike the old "Jack-the-Ripper" tragedies,' Brown remarked.

'Yes, there is some similarity, only his victims were women,' Rhymer observed, 'but in this case they are men, and it's significant to note that they were young and active as well.'

'Which looks as though the murderer possessed considerable muscular strength, and audacity into the bargain—'

'Hulloa! What's this?' Rhymer suddenly interrupted, coming to a standstill and gazing straight in front of him.

Brown hurriedly glanced in the same direction, where he beheld a blurred figure rapidly approaching them along the narrow lane. It was about fifty yards ahead. The midsummer twilight was rapidly fading, so it was difficult to see clearly at that distance. Its general aspect, however, was so forbidding, that Rhymer grasped the detective sharply by the arm and dragged him into a gap in the hedge, at the same time motioning him to silence.

They were only just in time, for a moment or two later the object was alongside their hiding-place, thus enabling them to obtain a clearer vision of it without being observed themselves.

This transitory view, as the figure shot past them, was far from reassuring. As they crouched there, an unaccountable sense of chilliness was prevalent. Brown afterwards owned up to an uncontrollable feeling of nausea as he beheld the figure. The unearthly face conveyed features devilish in their cold and pitiless cruelty, lifeless in their immobility, vacant in their utter lack of human expression – lifeless, yet living. The eyes were lack-lustre, yet wide open and round. The figure resembled that of a male, judging by its height and build. It was hatless and enveloped in a long cloak, from the folds of which an emaciated hand protruded – grasping a long, gleaming knife.

As the Creature swept past, a fetid, pungent smell was evident – horribly nauseous and corrupt.

Almost directly after the Thing had passed their place of

concealment, Rhymer sprang into the lane.

'Come along,' he urged in a loud whisper, 'as quietly as you can. We mustn't lose sight of it.' Then, setting off after the retreating figure, beckoned Brown to follow.

The detective was middle-aged, stout and out of training, whereas Rhymer was lean and agile. As a consequence, he soon outdistanced the former, resulting in him and the object of his chase shortly being hidden from the detective by a sharp bend in the lane.

A few moments later, Brown was alarmed by the sudden report of a shot, followed by a hoarse cry for help. Redoubling his efforts he was soon round the aforementioned bend, and there, a few yards in front, he beheld two figures sprawling in the middle of the lane.

As he hastened to the spot where they were struggling, his ears were assailed by a sound like that of a ferocious animal when worrying its prey. Then the figure that was uppermost in the scrimmage suddenly sprang up, and turning upon the detective a ghastly face, distorted with the fierce passion of blood-lust, revealed the repulsive features of the Creature they were pursuing. With an indescribable, sickening, voiceless wail – which, somehow, seemed to give expression to anguish born of ungratified desire – it sprang, with one frenzied leap, over the hedge and disappeared.

Quickly approaching the other figure, which lay in a

motionless heap upon the road, Brown beheld the limp form of the professor. Gently raising him, he was infinitely relieved to see him open his eyes.

He sighed audibly, and then stared with a dazed expression. In less than a moment, however, full consciousness returned. A flashing light of comprehension shone in his eyes as he regarded his rescuer.

'Have you collared it?' he cried.

'If you mean the thing that's just attacked you, I haven't.'

'You don't mean to say that devil's given us the slip?'

'I'm sorry, sir, but the brute was one too many for both of us; it jumped clean over the hedge before one could say "Jack Robinson"; but I hope you're not seriously hurt?'

'I shall be all right in a few minutes; but it's a confounded nuisance that "freak" 's got away,' said he, looking far more annoyed than injured. Raising his hand he placed the tips of his fingers upon his neck for a moment, and as he withdrew them Brown observed they were smeared with blood. Glancing with a thrill of apprehension at Rhymer's neck, he observed two small incisions from which a slight stream of blood was slowly oozing.

'Good heavens!' he exclaimed, 'your injury's similar to those of the three Blankborough victims; only, thank goodness, you've escaped with your life and any, more serious, wounds.'

'Your arrival, undoubtedly, saved me from a loathsome death, and butchery as well,' he replied as he took a white silk handkerchief from his pocket and deftly bound it round his neck, adding, 'Then you didn't come to grips with that fiend?'

'No, for the beggar bolted directly it saw me, before I had a chance even of attempting to seize it. What was the shot I heard?' he added.

'The report of my automatic pistol, and the strange thing is, I plugged the beggar at close quarters, clean through the body – impossible to have missed at such a close range – just as it tackled me – the moment I rounded the bend in the lane, where it had apparently halted.'

'Didn't attempt to stab you with that knife it carried?'

'That's the remarkable thing about it,' he replied. 'The Creature – who possessed abnormal strength – made one spring and floored me, at the same time dropping the knife, which fell with a clatter upon the road. Then it pinned me firmly down with its hands and knees and bent its face close to mine. I was quite helpless in its grasp. It bared its fangs with a snarl, and deliberately bit me in the neck. I was speechless for the moment with horror, but by a supreme effort I succeeded in raising a cry for help, though the exertion proved too much and I lost consciousness.'

'It's evident you've narrowly escaped the fate of those other poor fellows. Great Scot, it was a near shave! Here, take a pull at this,' he added, producing a flask from his pocket.

The stimulant rapidly revived Rhymer.

'Thanks,' he exclaimed, returning the flask. 'That's better. Now we must be getting on, for there's no time to be lost if we are to follow up this clue.'

'Anyhow, we've had a glimpse of the criminal we're after, that's very evident,' Brown asserted, 'and we shall both be able to swear to its identity, since I, for one, shall never forget the features of that monstrosity, if I live to be a hundred. Besides, since you say you've lodged a bullet in its carcase, it's not likely to travel far. We had better search over the hedge yonder.'

'You're free to search to your heart's content, but I'm going straight back to the hotel to cauterize and dress this bite in my neck.'

Brown looked askance at this remark, which was uttered with a trace of petulance.

'This thing cannot be dealt with by the customary CID methods,' Rhymer went on to explain, 'for I'm convinced that neither powder and shot nor even cold steel will have any effect in the ultimate capture of this Living-death, which you vainly hope to find over that hedge. Neither would your steel bracelets have any purchase upon its wrists. We're up against something abnormal here, and we must cut our coat according to our cloth.'

Brown at first appeared a trifle crestfallen, after listening to these disparaging comments upon his latest suggestion. The extraordinary circumstances sorely puzzled him, but he had the intuition to realize that some influence outside the usual rut of criminal investigation was facing them, and being previously assured of Rhymer's experience in such matters, was content to be guided by him, at any rate for the present.

'I'm blessed if I can follow the hang of the thing,' Brown grumbled, 'for I had labelled your assailant as a dangerous lunatic at large. Your last remark, however, puts quite another complexion on the matter.'

'You detectives are such a hidebound crowd,' Rhymer remarked with an indulgent smile, 'you try to handcuff clues as well as criminals. Give me plenty of scope when hot upon a clue, then I can forge ahead unencumbered.'

'Have you any definite clue, sir, to follow?'

'Yes, Brown, I've three. First, there are the incisions in my neck; secondly, there is this,' and displaying the palm of his right hand, exhibited a fragment of dark cloth, which, from its frayed appearance, had evidently been torn from some garment in the recent struggle. 'And here is the third,' he added, betraying a note of triumph, as, taking a few steps, he stooped and picked up an object lying at the side of the road.

'Ah! the assassin's knife,' Brown exclaimed.

'Precisely, and it's probably the identical weapon with which those poor chaps' bodies were so hacked about, so it's an important link in our chain of evidence.'

'And a deucedly significant one, too,' Brown added.

There was the twinkle of a smile in Rhymer's eyes as he enquired:

'Are you still inclined to search for your escaped lunatic over the hedge, or shall we return to our quarters?'

The detective stiffened as he replied:

'It's my duty as an officer of the law to let no chance slip by, my professional credit's at stake, remember; but I am quite willing to be guided by you – especially as I asked for your assistance.'

'And you are welcome to it, Brown, as well as all the official credit, if success crowns our efforts. But I must ask you to act upon the lines that I point out. Is that agreed?'

'Quite, sir, and with your acumen you will be certain to find out something further that will help us to bottom this mystery after all.'

'Hope I may, Brown, I'm sure; so let's turn in for the night. I'm feeling a bit fagged after my wrestling-bout with that anaemic-looking blighter.'

'Hope you're feeling no worse, sir, after last night's

experiences,' the detective enquired the following morning when he and Rhymer met at breakfast.

'I'm as fit as a fiddle, thanks,' said he; 'a good night's rest works wonders. It takes a lot to keep me awake long, when once I'm between the sheets.'

'How's your neck?' the detective added, glancing at a neat strip of sticking-plaster covering the injured part.

'Oh, just a trifle sore, that's all. The incisions weren't deep. I cauterized them last night, so don't contemplate any trouble in that direction.'

After breakfast they adjourned to the privacy of Rhymer's bedroom in order to map out future plans. During their discussion he produced the incriminating knife, and, handing it to Brown, remarked:

'Quite an antique, eh?'

The latter examined it with keen interest.

'Evidently,' said he, 'but its age doesn't lessen the cutthroat appearance of the engraven blade, set in its massive handle. A remarkable tool, I must admit, resembling, more than anything I've ever seen, a Kukri, the Gurka fighting weapon. One thing's evident, though—'

'What's that?' Rhymer interrupted.

'Why, that it belongs to the ugly brute we fell foul of last night.'

'Sorry to disagree with you,' said Rhymer, 'but we have

yet to discover the real owner of this piece of cutlery, and until that's accomplished we're a long way off a solution of the mystery.'

Brown, unconvinced, shook his head.

'Well, it's beyond me even to guess what you're driving at. Anyhow, the weapon was owned by that individual temporarily – we can both swear to that – and possession is nine points of the law.'

'I shouldn't try and guess, if I were you,' Rhymer advised. 'Guessing is always destructive to logic. Far better observe small facts upon which large impressions may depend.'

'Then *you* haven't any idea as to whom else this knife may belong?'

'Not the vaguest.'

'And yet you refuse to believe it belongs to the creature who dropped it?'

'That's my opinion.'

'It's all an insoluble mystery to me,' said Brown, 'it gets thicker instead of clearer.'

'On the contrary,' Rhymer contradicted, 'it clears every instant.'

'Then, hang it all, sir, can't you help me out of the fog?'

'That's what I'm trying to do.'

'How?'

'By taking steps to discover the owner of the knife, of

course. I wonder if our landlord has an up-to-date copy of the local directory? I'll go and find out.'

Subsequent enquiry produced a recent edition of this book, and for the next few minutes they were poring over its pages.

It contained the customary list of private and commercial residents. Among the former, one name attracted Rhymer's attention:

'Ludwig Holtsner. The Gables.'

'An enemy in our midst,' he exclaimed, pointing it out to Brown. 'That fellow ought to have been interned.'

'He's bound to be naturalized,' the detective replied.

'All the more suspicious and dangerous. If I had my way, all Boche-born individuals residing in this country – notwithstanding their naturalization – should be interned. Boches will be Boches, and a mere scrap of paper, identifying them as naturalized British subjects, won't wipe out the inherited taint of *Kultur*. I don't trust the breed, and when I come across a male or female Boche my suspicions are instantly aroused.'

'We keep a sharp enough eye upon any suspicious characters of that sort,' Brown affirmed a trifle aggressively – so Rhymer thought.

'I'm not casting any slur upon the efficacy of the police in their dealings with aliens, but even they have been gulled by the Hun, over here, more than once.'

'I didn't suggest you were, sir, but we often get blame we don't deserve, so we are bound to drop an occasional word of protest.'

'I'm not contesting your rights in that direction, Brown.'

'All right, sir, but I like to justify my assertions, so I'll just slip round to the police station and hear what the local superintendent has to say about this Ludwig Holtsner. He won't have failed to make full enquiries, I know.'

'An excellent idea, Brown, only take care not to say a word about our adventure last night, since secrecy regarding our actions – for the present – will best promote our chance of ultimate success.'

'Very good, sir.'

Half an hour later Brown returned, having achieved his visit to the police station.

'Well, obtained any useful information?' Rhymer enquired.

'Not much in support of your suspicion, anyhow, regarding this Mr Holtsner,' he replied. 'The superintendent told me that he took out naturalization papers many years ago, and is quite all right. A man of local influence – he hastened to assure me – a wealthy bachelor and occupying a large house which he purchased.'

'Any other particulars?'

'Nothing of much importance, I imagine.'

'Did the superintendent say how Holtsner occupied his time?'

'Oh yes, he studied science a lot and was quite a keen Egyptologist.'

Rhymer's eyes sparkled as he heard this last piece of information. Instantly his faculties were on the alert.

'They are all quite all right until they're caught red-handed. And then – well – there's the very devil to pay. But, at all events, you've brought back one valuable piece of evidence in support of a theory I've already broached.'

'Oh! What's that?'

'My dear Inspector, do try a little analysis yourself,' he enjoined with a touch of impatience. 'I've already given you some broad hints as to my methods. Now it's up to you to apply them.'

Brown looked distinctly piqued.

'Very well, sir, as you choose to put it in that fashion. I've nothing more to say—'

'Which will afford you a better opportunity for mental analysis,' Rhymer chipped in with an apologetic smile. 'And may I give you a golden rule which I was taught by a famous detective?' He paused for a reply.

'Get on with it, then.'

'Well, when you have worn out the possible, whatever is

left, however impossible, comes mighty near the truth.'

No place can be more productive of local information than the bar-parlour of a country town hotel. Brown was keenly alive to this fact, and that was why he got Rhymer to join him in the bar of the King's Arms later on in the day.

'We may pick up some useful information here, sir, if we keep our eyes and ears open.'

'A suggestion full of possibilities, Brown, so let's pledge our success in a drop of dry ginger. Can't make it anything stronger, if I'm to stand treat. It's forbidden by D.O.R.A. – And you are one of her guardians.'

They had been silently smoking for some little time, when two men entered the room, which was fairly full. They sat down at a vacant table next to that at which Rhymer and Brown were seated.

Having called for some liquid refreshment, they opened a brisk conversation. Their general appearance plainly identified them as men-servants, who had dropped in at their favourite house of call for a friendly chat over the cup that cheers and loosens the tongue.

'Well, Alf,' the taller of the two was heard by their neighbours to remark, 'how's your governor been treating you of late?'

'Not 'alf, Jim,' was the reply. ''E's balmy, 'e is. I tell yer it's fair getting on my nerves.'

'Why, wot's 'e been a-doing of now, Alf – anything fresh?'

'Fresh!' he reiterated disdainfully. 'Not much – same old row, blaming me for things I 'ain't done. That's all.'

'Wot 'aven't yer done?'

'Nothing. It's 'im 'as done it. Gone and lost a bloomin' old knife that belonged to some 'eathen wot lived 'undreds of years ago – says it's worth pots of money, and because 'e can't find it, swears I've pinched it. I like 'is cheek.'

At this point their conversation was interrupted by the arrival of a third man who joined them, and a few moments later, after draining their glasses, they left the bar together.

Rhymer casually arose and, strolling across to the counter, addressed the barmaid behind:

'Can you tell me, Miss, who those two men were, sitting at the table next to ours? They've just left with a friend.'

'Yes, sir,' she replied with a glance of slight enquiry, 'the short one was James Smith, a footman at Sir William Doone's, and the other Alfred Ball, valet to Mr Holtsner.'

'Thanks,' said he, 'then I'm mistaken. One of them reminded me of a servant that left me some years ago,' he mendaciously added, to ease her mind of any faint suspicion he might have aroused as to the real reason of his enquiry.

A few minutes later, Rhymer and Brown were again closeted in the former's bedroom.

'We're progressing like a house on fire,' the former affirmed, rubbing his hands. 'You overheard what that fellow said about the knife? Well, the barmaid confirmed my suspicion that he was a servant of Holtsner's, so now it's pretty evident to whom the knife belongs.'

'Quite clear,' said Brown, 'and you were right after all. We may also take it that the knife was stolen from The Gables by that blooming chump we met in the lane, and without Holtsner's knowledge, too.'

'That's more than probable, and I'll go a step further in suggesting that Holtsner's not entirely ignorant of this Creature's presence in the locality, although he may not be actually aware it was the thief, since then he would scarcely have blamed Alfred Ball for his loss. Still, it must be remembered that a man, being acquainted with anything abnormal haunting his premises, usually wants to hush it up, since it gives the place a bad name.'

'Quite so,' said Brown. 'Yet there's something more beneath than meets the eye; although I admit the fog's clearing a bit.'

'Suspicions are becoming certainties, you mean,' Rhymer added. 'But, look here, we mustn't lose another minute. It's now six-thirty,' consulting his watch, 'and we've got to visit this German fellow as soon as possible, under cover of some pretext or other. Our episode in finding the knife is a good enough excuse for calling, even at this hour, in order to restore it to him.'

'That will also place him under an obligation,' said Brown, 'which may help matters forward a bit.'

'That's quite probable.'

'Do you know whereabouts his house is?' Brown enquired after a pause.

'Yes, I asked the landlord when returning the directory. It's not more than a quarter of an hour's walk, so let's get off.'

'We shall need extra caution at this stage,' Rhymer remarked, as they were hurrying along the lane which they had traversed the previous night. 'I'm positive it would be wiser for me to call on Holtsner alone, until I discover how the land lies; so I hope you won't mind waiting for me outside. We must avoid exciting this man's suspicion, and if we both arrive together he might suspect the real object of our visit.'

He spoke with a seriousness which gave authority to his words.

At first Brown seemed inclined to protest, but after a little consideration, fell in with the proposition.

'I'm sure I am advising you for the best,' Rhymer remarked as he halted opposite a pair of massive, iron gates guarding a long and tortuous drive. 'This is The Gables, I expect,' he added. 'If I should fail to return within – say – half an hour, you'd better call for me.'

With this parting injunction he entered the drive and soon disappeared round a curve in the shrub-lined avenue.

Arriving at the house, he was admitted by a man-servant whom he recognized as Alfred Ball.

'I've called to see Mr Holtsner,' said he, presenting his card, 'kindly inform him it's a matter of business.'

'I'm not sure if the master's at home, sir,' was the noncommittal reply, 'but I'll enquire if you'll please step inside.'

He then conducted him to a small room at the further end of the hall.

A few minutes later the door opened, and a tall, middle-aged man entered, of fair complexion with closely-cropped hair and a bristly moustache.

He was inclined to obesity and wore a pair of gold-rimmed spectacles fitted with powerful lenses, which accentuated the prominency of his protruding eyes.

He bowed to his visitor, exclaiming in a deep, guttural voice – as he glanced at the visiting card held between his podgy thumb and forefinger:

'Professor Rhymer, I presume?'

'That is my name, Mr Holtsner,' he replied as he mentally sized up the fat German. 'I must apologize for this late call, but I've found an article which I believe you've had stolen,' handing him a brown-paper parcel.

Holtsner took it with a look of blank enquiry, and proceeded to remove the paper, exclaiming:

'Something I've had stolen – what can it be – er – where did you find it?'

'In the lane outside your drive.'

'In the lane—' Holtsner reiterated, pausing all of a sudden – arrested by the discovery of the knife which the parcel now disclosed.

'Well – how on earth—' he continued with an apparent effort, but the remainder of his speech died away upon his lips as he glanced suspiciously at the professor.

Rhymer met his look squarely with a well-feigned expression of innocent surprise, as though at a loss to account for his hesitation.

'You were going to say, Mr Holtsner, "how on earth did I guess that this interesting antique belonged to you?" ' he suggested with a frank smile. 'Well, I can soon satisfy you upon that score, for I chanced to overhear some one casually remark that you had lost a valuable knife, and as I had previously happened to stumble across one in the lane, whilst enjoying a stroll, I thought I'd call and enquire if it was yours. If it's not, then I'd better leave it at the police station.'

This assumption of candour seemed to reassure Holtsner.

'Yes, this belongs to me; it was stolen from my museum,' he acknowledged somewhat reluctantly; 'but who did you overhear say I'd lost it?'

'Excuse me, sir, but it would hardly be fair for me to say, since the information was not intended for my ears. I only overheard it by chance.'

Holtsner was on the verge of resenting Rhymer's refusal to satisfy his enquiry, but he evidently thought better of it, apologetically exclaiming:

'Quite so, I oughtn't to have asked. I'm a keen collector of antiques, and was put out at losing this valuable relic of a lost Egyptian art. Its sudden recovery flustered me, so pray accept my apologies and thanks as well, for what you've done. By the way,' he added with assumed unconcern, 'you don't happen to have mentioned the matter to the police?'

'No,' said Rhymer.

'Ah! it's just as well you didn't,' said he, with an involuntary sigh of relief. 'You see, I suspect one of my servants of the theft, and I've no wish to prosecute. The police are so officious in these matters – I'm sure you'll understand?'

'Perfectly,' was the response.

It was evident to Rhymer's keen sense of observation that Holtsner's apparent agitation was not solely due to the cause he so lamely advanced. There was something he was anxious to hide. The man might be a collector, in fact, the local superintendent of police had informed Brown that such was the case; but the loss of a valuable antique and its subsequent restoration by a stranger, who had simply picked it up upon the road, would hardly account for its owner appearing as disturbed as Holtsner seemed to be.

His very attitude invited suspicion, but Rhymer was cute enough to conceal any trace of his conviction that Holtsner was playing a deep game; so, assuming an attitude of nonchalance, said:

'I'm awfully glad I've found your knife, since it's afforded me the privilege of making your acquaintance, and being a scientist and collector myself, it's a pleasure to meet others with similar tastes.'

Rhymer's diplomatic reply seemed to set the German's suspicions at rest, for he enquired:

'Are you staying long in the neighbourhood?'

'Only a few days. I've run down with a friend from town to make a geological survey.'

Rhymer invented this excuse on the spur of the moment, since he judged it would avert further suspicion that might arise in Holtsner's mind, should he come across him and Brown roaming about the vicinity.

'An attractive branch of science,' said Holtsner, 'and it may interest you to know that I have some geological specimens found in the neighbourhood, which I'd like to show you in my museum.'

That was just what Rhymer desired. He didn't care a rap about the specimens, but he did want to get into the museum. So, without displaying any sign of the satisfaction he felt, replied:

'Thanks, I *should* like to see these specimens; but I fear I can't stop now. I'm overdue to join my friend at our hotel, but as he is also keen on geology, may I bring him along as well? Shall we say tomorrow?'

'By all means. How would the morning suit you? I'm a man of leisure, so my time's at your convenience.'

'That'll do admirably,' he replied, and, bidding his host goodbye, took his departure, rejoining Brown a few minutes later in the lane.

'Thought you were never coming,' was the detective's greeting. 'I was going to call for you in another minute. You've exceeded your time-limit and I was beginning to get anxious.'

'It's fortunate you didn't; as it was, I had some difficulty in getting away when I did, and if you had suddenly turned up we should have been in the deuce of a mess. So far I've fixed things up all right. The man acknowledges he's the owner of the knife, and though he seemed suspicious at first, I think I succeeded in blinding him as to the purpose of my visit. Told him I was down here with a friend to make a geological survey. He seemed to swallow the fable readily enough, and invited me to look at a museum he has on the premises. I'd have liked to go, there and then, but the event of your sudden appearance upon the scene – as requested – precluded my doing so. I got him, however, to ask the two of us to see the museum tomorrow morning.'

Brown pondered a few moments.

'That's top hole,' he at length exclaimed, 'for now we may be able to pick up some evidence in that place.'

'Exactly what I hope to do, for he let out that the knife was stolen from it.'

'Then in all probability the assassin will have left some traces there – finger marks or similar clues,' Brown hazarded.

'I hope to find something more tangible than that.'

'Hang it all, sir, what more could you find without you knocked up against the actual criminal?'

'Nothing whatever.'

Brown stared at his collaborator, and was on the point of making some further remark when he suddenly remembered the professor's former tip – 'Try and do a little analysis yourself' – so he tried and relapsed into silence.

'By the way,' Rhymer presently enquired, 'do you know anything about geology?'

'Well – yes – a trifle. I studied it a little in my school days; but I've only a very hazy recollection of the subject now.'

'No matter, all I want you to do is to make out you're keen on the thing when we visit Holtsner tomorrow morning.'

In due course Rhymer and Brown turned up at The Gables, and were courteously received by Holtsner. Without wasting any time, their host led them into the museum – a large and lofty apartment built off from the house, though connected by a short passage with a door at either end.

Brown no sooner entered this apartment than he experienced a sensation of vague, unaccountable horror. A conviction of some eerie presence gripped tight hold of him. He advanced into the centre of the room, still oppressed with this novel sensation, which increased rather than diminished. He was no coward, neither was he superstitious, so the horror which obsessed him was all the more apprehensive.

Suddenly his gaze was attracted by a row of mummy cases which stood on end in a long showcase – fitted with glass doors – extending the full length of one end of the building.

He stared, awe-inspired, at the row of garishly-painted wooden boxes, containing their human relics of a bygone age. The lid of one was open, disclosing a swathed and bandaged form. Its lofty cheek bones, massive jaw, and aquiline nose depicted power and diffused a subtle influence – a latent force which was indefinable.

'My Egyptian mummies seem to interest you, sir,' Holtsner

exclaimed, mistaking the keen attention Brown bestowed upon these curiosities as indicating admiration rather than horror.

'They're apt to give one the creeps,' he replied with an effort to hide his uneasiness, 'but that object in the open box seems to be in good condition—'

'What on earth do you know, Brown, about the condition of mummies?' Rhymer suddenly interrupted, giving the detective a warning look, unobserved by Holtsner. 'Geology is more in your line, so, for goodness' sake, stick to it and don't air your views upon matters you know nothing about.'

'What do you know about mummies?' Brown retorted.

'Not much,' said Rhymer, flashing him another significant glance, 'but sufficient to convince me the Egyptian lady or gentleman in that box is as old as Adam and not any better preserved than the majority of its class.'

'Professor Rhymer is quite right,' Holtsner was quick to assert, with what appeared to Rhymer undue emphasis; 'all these mummies date back to a remote Egyptian dynasty; but,' he added with precipitancy, 'as you and your friend are keen on geological specimens, if you'll look at this case over here, you'll find some fossils of local interest.'

'Ah, that's more in our line, Brown, isn't it?' said Rhymer as he moved towards his host, followed by the detective.

The specimens indicated were mainly echinoderms,

lamellibranchs, and gasteropods, which were neatly labelled and displayed in glass cases. While they were inspecting these, Holtsner moved away in another direction in order to pick up some object off a table, apart from where they had all been standing.

Rhymer seized this opportunity to whisper into the detective's ear:

'For heaven's sake, man, don't allude again to those mummies, but do try and feign some sort of enthusiasm over these blessed fossils.' Then, raising his voice for Holtsner's benefit, exclaimed:

'What a topping specimen of the *Tritonium corrugatum*! Observe the fusiform shell – the elongated spire and the slightly curved anterior canal. The gasteropods are very beautiful. Well, I fear we must be making a move if we are to get to town in time for that lecture tonight, and I don't want to miss it. I've some letters to get off, too, before we leave by the afternoon train.'

Holtsner overheard these remarks, as Rhymer intended he should, and as he again approached his guests, a look of satisfaction overspread his features.

'Jolly fine collection of yours, Mr Holtsner,' Rhymer enthusiastically observed, 'sorry we must be going – awfully obliged to you for showing us round. Quite envy you the possession of such a museum.'

'Pray don't mention it, sir; only too delighted, I'm sure. It's a pleasure to show one's things to those who can appreciate them. Hope you and your friend will drop in again, when you've more time at your disposal.'

'I can promise you that much,' was Rhymer's unspoken comment, 'only the visit will be a strictly private one, as far as your knowledge is concerned.' Then aloud he exclaimed:

'Many thanks, some day we may, I hope, have another look round.'

As soon as Rhymer and the detective had left The Gables, the former exclaimed:

'By Jove! But you made an unfortunate remark about that mummy, and, unwittingly – I presume – stumbled nearer the truth than you had any idea of. Holtsner, too, pricked up his ears. You kind of "put the wind up him", as the "Tommies" say. However, I doubt if any real harm's done, since he appeared somewhat reassured after I'd chipped in with my contradictory remark.'

'Whatever are you driving at?' Brown exclaimed, apparently nettled.

'Wait till you and I have got into that museum alone – which we must do tonight by hook or by crook – and then you'll know. We've got to fix up a private view of those mummies. I've made it pretty clear to the Boche, our professed intention of going to London this afternoon, and though he's still inclined to suspicion, I think we've managed fairly to mislead him with regard to our interest in his mummies. Anyhow, he won't be expecting us back in Biankborough until tomorrow, and that's a feather in the cap of our plan.'

After lunch Rhymer and Brown left the hotel for the station, with a handbag apiece, in order to convey the impression they were off for the night. Upon their arrival at the booking-office, Rhymer loudly demanded two tickets for Charing Cross. Having entered a first-class smoker and finding themselves alone, Brown remarked:

'You seemed anxious to let everybody know where we were going, sir, by the way you yelled out for the tickets.'

'Not every one, Brown – only Ball, Holtsner's servant, whom I spotted spying upon us – as he imagined unobserved – from behind a barrow piled up with luggage. I warned you that the Boche was still suspicious. Now he'll soon be posted up with the information that we have cleared out, with our kit, for a night in town.'

As the train approached the next station – three miles from Biankborough – Rhymer abruptly signified that it was to be their destination. A few minutes later they were out on the platform. Then, without any further word of explanation, Rhymer set off at a leisurely pace along the road, in the direction from which they had just come, with Brown –

looking annoyed and puzzled – following in his wake.

The former volunteered no explanation until they arrived opposite a stile, where he suddenly halted.

'We'll take it easy for a bit here. Hope you've brought your pipe, Brown? Then let's light up, for on no account must we turn up at Blankborough again before dusk.'

The museum attached to The Gables had two entrances. One leading from the house, through which Holtsner had conducted his visitors that morning, the other giving access from the garden.

Outside the latter entrance – in the evening – Rhymer and Brown, concealed behind a thick bush, were watching the door, which was slightly ajar.

Suddenly the former slipped from his hiding-place – motioning the detective to remain where he was – and advanced on tiptoe towards the entrance.

Upon arriving there, he glued his eye to the chink between the hinges, intently observing something within. His inspection appeared to afford him satisfaction, judging by his expression when he subsequently returned to the seclusion of the bush.

'Sure enough, we're on the right track,' he whispered. 'Pay careful attention to what I'm going to say now.'

'I'm listening, sir.'

'At any moment a figure may slip out of that door, closely

resembling the freak we saw the night before last. Follow it, only keep at a safe distance, to avoid being seen if possible.'

Brown stifled an exclamation, and as a ray of moonlight struck his face, forcing its way through an aperture in the bush, Rhymer detected an expression akin to fear. Then with a challenging glance the former asserted:

'I'm no coward, sir, and I've yet to meet the crook I wouldn't tackle – provided it's human – but to stand up against a fiend like the one that went for you the other night – well – it's a bit more than I bargained for.'

'Don't blame you either, but so far my investigations give me confidence in assuming that as long as you don't directly impede this Creature's progress, it won't attack you. Follow at a safe distance and watch, that's all I ask you to do. I don't think *I* should have been mauled the other night had I not mentally registered a determination to go for the brute. My intentions were apparently conveyed by telepathy to the Creature's system of comprehension, hence the "scrap", which proved a "knock-out" for me.'

A creaking sound in the direction of the museum caused both men to turn round sharply, and there, illuminated by a ray of light from the now wide-opened door, a figure glided into the moonlight without.

'Quick!' Rhymer exclaimed with bated breath, 'don't lose sight of it.'

With a sharp intaking of breath, Brown started in pursuit, keeping his distance as directed, while Rhymer, with one rapid glance around, slipped through the open door of the museum.

Within the threshold he halted, as his eyes fell upon a recumbent figure stretched on a couch, over which a shaded electric lamp was burning, suspended from the vaulted ceiling.

Approaching on tiptoe, he recognized Holtsner. The German appeared to be in a deep sleep. A closer examination, however, revealed the man to be in a sort of trance, for his breathing was imperceptible. But for the faint trace of colour in his face, he might have been dead.

Rhymer then produced a small pocket mirror, and, placing it close to the man's nostrils, observed a slight blur on the surface. With a nod of satisfaction he replaced the glass in his pocket and was about to make a further inspection of the apartment, when his attention was suddenly arrested by the sound of stealthy footsteps in the passage that connected the museum with the house.

In a flash he surveyed his surroundings, and, spotting a curtained recess in the wall nearest him, slipped within. He had barely covered his retreat when the door slowly opened and some one entered whom he recognized – through a small rent in the curtain – as Alfred Ball.

The latter carefully closed the door behind him and locked it. Next he cautiously approached the couch upon which his master lay, as if anxious to avoid disturbing him. Bestowing a cursory glance at the sleeper, he fetched a small table from another part of the room, placing it by the couch. Going to a cabinet he produced two stoppered bottles and a graduated glass measure, which he laid on the table by Holtsner's side. Then he crossed to another cupboard from which he took a coil of stout cord. Retaining this, he placed a chair close to the outer door – which was still slightly ajar – and sat down, with his head thrown forward, in an attitude of alertness.

About ten minutes later, without any warning, the door was violently flung back, and in rushed a figure which Rhymer recognized to be the one he and Brown had previously seen leaving the museum.

Its eyes were lit up with a fierce passion. The lips and chin daubed with blood – fresh blood – hardly yet dry. It made straight for the couch upon which Holtsner was lying, and in another moment, would have reached him, had not Ball sprung up and whisked the cord – which was fitted with a running noose – neatly over the Creature's head, fetching it, with a smart jerk, sprawling on the floor.

Simultaneously with the crash occasioned by the falling body, Holtsner languidly raised himself, stretching his arms; and, as he moved, the monster – struggling violently on the floor, hampered by the coils of the lasso – became motionless – a horrid, inert mass of bone and sinew.

Holtsner wearily dragged himself into a sitting posture and, leaning towards the table, poured out a few drops of liquid from each of the two bottles into the glass measure, and, with a trembling hand, tossed the stuff down his throat.

'That's better, Otto,' he gasped. 'These frequent trances are beginning to take it out of me.'

'Number two has strafed another enemy of the Fatherland,' the servant vehemently asserted, his features fairly distorted with 'Hate'. 'Look! there's the blood of some pig-swine on its lips.'

The two wretches were conversing in German, a language with which Rhymer was well acquainted. He was not a little surprised to discover that Ball was a Boche, for his cockney accent and speech, when recently in the King's Arms, were so perfectly assumed. But, when he gathered, from their recent remarks, that another murder had undoubtedly been committed, he became intensely anxious about Brown; and keen though he was to see what else Holtsner and his accomplice were up to, he inwardly raved to get away and find out where the inspector might be.

'Must stick where I am for the present,' he soliloquized, 'until those two devils clear out. Confound it all! I do hope poor Brown's all right.'

Meanwhile, Holtsner and Otto (to give the latter his correct name) set about a very revolting performance. A basin of water and a sponge were first produced, with which Otto, kneeling on the floor, carefully removed the bloodstains from the jaws of the motionless Thing lying there.

He then approached the large case with the glass doors – in which the mummies were stored – and, lifting out one of the tawdry Egyptian death-boxes, which was empty, laid it, with Holtsner's assistance, upon the floor. Opening the lid, they proceeded to place the inanimate Creature within, having first removed the lasso. Shutting down the hinged lid, they locked it, and, lifting the case between them, deposited it in its former place. Crossing the apartment to a small steel safe let into the wall, Holtsner unlocked the door, taking from within a leather notebook. Opening it he made an entry with a fountain pen.

He then put it back in the safe and began a rapid conversation with Otto, but their voices were so low that Rhymer was unable to hear what they said.

However, he was not kept much longer in suspense, for after stowing away the several articles they had been using, and carefully scrutinizing the apartment to make sure nothing incriminating was left about, they left the museum by the door communicating with the house, having first switched off the electric light.

Rhymer lost no time in quitting his cramped quarters. Noiselessly crossing the floor, he slipped back the latch of the garden door, opened it, and, as he bolted out, suddenly found himself confronted by a figure.

'Great Scot! How you startled me, Brown,' he exclaimed, upon discovering he had barged into the burly figure of the detective, 'how long have you been here?'

'For some little while, and I've seen what's been going on inside there, through a chink in the door. But where on earth have you been? I didn't see you in the place.'

'I was there right enough, concealed behind a curtain, where, like you, I could see without being seen. I'm glad you saw this sickening spectacle, since a witness will be useful. Why didn't you follow up the Thing as I asked?'

'I did my best, but It was too much for me. I couldn't keep up the pace. Lor'! how the Thing did scoot. Lost sight of it at the high boundary wall – topped with broken glass – which encloses the grounds. It scaled this with perfect ease, though it was too high for me to attempt. There I remained on the look-out for about a quarter of an hour, when I suddenly spotted it again doubling back on its original tracks. So, quickly hiding behind the trunk of a tree until it had passed, I followed it back here again. Had it not been for the bright moonlight, I couldn't have done as much as I did – but preserve me from ever seeing a sight like that in the museum again.'

'Quite Teutonic, wasn't it?'

'Teutonic? Why, I call it diabolical.'

'The same thing,' Rhymer observed. 'Anyhow you did your best, but I fear we shall shortly hear of another of these wretched murders as a result of tonight's work. You've got your electric torch and some skeleton keys, haven't you?'

'Yes, I have.'

'Good, then we'll proceed without delay. There's some more evidence I'm anxious to secure in there,' he added, nodding in the direction of the museum. 'I daren't switch on the light, as they might see the reflection from the house. There's a safe inside we must investigate. Quite an ordinary affair, I imagine, so one of your skeleton keys should fix up the job.'

It transpired as Rhymer had predicted. The safe was soon opened and the notebook produced. With the aid of Brown's torch they examined the contents. It proved to be a ruled manuscript, only just commenced. Some brief instructions, written in a German fist, occupied the first two or three pages.

Brown didn't know any German, but Rhymer was able to read the contents. It only took him a few minutes, and as he proceeded, first bewilderment, and then horror gripped him. Turning, at length, to Brown, he exclaimed:

'It's almost incredible! However, we've no time now to go into details. We must get away as quickly and quietly as possible. Every moment increases the risk of discovery.'

He then replaced the incriminating document in the safe and locked it.

Silently the two men left the chamber of mystery by the garden door, closing it carefully behind them. As they were walking to the inn, Rhymer suddenly exclaimed:

'It's amazing to think what fiends these Boches are. They'll stick at nothing. That book in the safe yonder contains some documentary evidence revealing one of the most revolting plots that could foul the imagination. Nothing short of *Kultur* – with a capital K – could hit upon such a conspiracy. Thank goodness, it's been our good luck to knock up against the thing in time, before these murders became wholesale, which, judging from the evidence, might shortly have been the case.'

'Good heavens! Do you mean to say that these Blankborough murders are part and parcel of a Boche conspiracy?'

'Undoubtedly that's the bald state of affairs, due, of course, to the tolerance of a naturalized enemy in our midst. And if we are to nip in the bud a scheme devised by demons in human form, we must lose no time in acquainting the authorities with our discovery. Yours is a name to conjure with at the "Yard": could you possibly get me a personal interview with your chief first thing tomorrow morning?'

'Then you believe Holtsner to be responsible for these murders?' Brown asked, evading the other question.

'Undoubtedly so; and for a good deal more besides.'

'Then he must be, somehow, employing demoniacal agencies?'

'That's more than probable, after what we've both witnessed.'

'Well, I'm jiggered! Can't understand it even now, but I can believe anything of the Boche, and though you've not yet told me all the details of the plot revealed in that book, I'm willing to phone to my chief and ask him to receive you as early as possible tomorrow morning.'

'Thanks,' was Rhymer's brief, but grateful response.

Brown's chief didn't appear very favourably disposed towards Rhymer as the latter was ushered at 8 a.m. the following morning into his sanctum at the 'Yard'.

'This is an extraordinarily early hour to fix for an interview, sir,' he curtly announced, as he motioned Rhymer to a chair. 'Your business must be correspondingly urgent, I presume.'

'Couldn't be more so.'

'Humph! Then I hope you'll waste no time in getting through with it. I'm up to my ears in work, and had it not been for Inspector Brown's urgent call upon the phone, I shouldn't have been here to meet you. I'm for ever being rung up to listen to matters of so-called "national importance" from unofficial quarters, which usually result in the discovery of a mare's nest.'

'I don't think you'll find my communication to be one of that sort, I only wish you might; besides, Inspector Brown can corroborate it.'

'So I understand. Please proceed, Professor Rhymer.'

Without further preamble he began to relate all that had occurred at Blankborough since his arrival there in Brown's company, including the evidence he had obtained from the notebook in Holtsner's safe.

The official listened attentively as Rhymer continued his narrative. He never once interrupted until the report was completed.

Then abruptly turning towards the professor, he exclaimed:

'This is indeed a serious matter, if you are correct in your allegations, but I can hardly believe it.'

'Surely, sir, nothing the Boche might do is beyond your powers of credibility?'

'Under the circumstances, I admit you have acted judiciously in reporting the matter so promptly,' said he, ignoring Rhymer's last remark, 'but it's scarcely comprehensible.'

'Anyhow, I've clearly stated the facts, sir.'

'I know, and I'm quite aware there's something out of the ordinary rut in these Blankborough crimes, and though I'm not predisposed to place much faith in psychological phenomena, you have certainly impressed me with your view of the matter.'

Just then the telephone on the chiefs desk rang up. He picked up the receiver and held it to his ear, thoughtfully replacing it a few moments later.

'These crimes are decidedly getting ahead of us. I've just received intimation of another murder last night at Blankborough, so your inference, sir, has been corroborated.'

Rhymer exhibited no surprise at this statement.

'It's only what I expected,' said he, 'and it supplements my plea for immediate and drastic measures.'

The official regarded him meditatively.

'May I make a suggestion?' Rhymer ventured.

'By all means.'

'Then, for goodness sake, sir, do use your influence to set the machinery in motion. Issue a confidential communication to every police centre throughout the British Isles, with instructions to furnish fresh reports relating to any naturalized Boches residing in each locality; especially ear-marking those engaged in scientific pursuits, and noting whether they are in possession of any Egyptian mummies. It would be well to insist upon all cargoes, shipped through neutral ports, being searched, and if any of these embalmed specimens are found on board, have them instantly confiscated as contraband. That would effectually put a stop to these atrocities.'

'I can see no difficulty in adopting the first part of your suggestion, but the latter might meet with serious obstacles.'

'Well, all I can say is that the safety of hundreds of human lives depends upon it.'

The chief fell to brooding again.

'Upon my word,' said he, 'I believe you're right, and I'm half inclined to try it – as far as it lies in my power; but others in authority will have to be consulted first.'

'I realized that from the commencement, but surely no responsible person in his right senses would hesitate to take prompt measures to quell a serious menace like this, for, should the German Intelligence Department get an inkling that we are on their tracks, all evidence would quickly be effaced by them.'

'That's very evident, but we must arrest this Holtsner fellow first.'

'Exactly: and if you'll give me a free hand, I'll undertake to catch him red-handed. Then you can more easily effect a wholesale arrest of naturalized Boches throughout the country on a charge of conspiracy, once their leader is safely under lock and key.'

'I'm relying a lot upon your assurances, Professor, and if you have made a blunder, then there'll be the deuce of a row.'

'I assure you I've made no mistake.'

'Well, I'll risk it.'

'And you'll let me have Brown's services for a little while longer at Blankborough?'

The chief pondered, and then with a look of resignation, said:

'Quite irregular, you know, since this case is officially in Brown's hands. It'll be creating a precedent, too. But the circumstances are exceptional, so I suppose I must agree.'

'Then Brown may return with me to Blankborough with a warrant for Holtsner's and Ball's arrest, and act under my directions?'

'Since you urge it, yes,' he reluctantly replied.

He pressed an electric push at the side of his desk, a plain-clothes officer shortly making his appearance.

'Tell Detective-Inspector Brown I want to see him.'

In a few moments the latter arrived.

'Professor Rhymer's officially assisting in the Blankborough murder case. You will return with him and work together until further notice.'

After leaving Scotland Yard, Rhymer and the detective entered the first small restaurant they came across.

'We can discuss some breakfast here, and our future plans into the bargain, for we appear to be the sole occupants,' Rhymer remarked as he sat down at a small table.

'Not a bad idea either, sir, a journey before breakfast gives one an appetite.'

'Our case is almost complete,' Rhymer affirmed after the waitress had departed with their order, 'but even now we mustn't err on the side of over-confidence.'

'I'm quite alive to that fact, sir.'

'I don't propose returning to Blankborough till later in the day. Then we'll hire a car and arrange to be dropped within easy walking distance of The Gables. After breakfast I want you to phone to the local superintendent at Blankborough, and get him to send two plain-clothes men to meet us at some convenient spot, which I'll leave you to fix up.'

'Very good, sir.'

'Be sure you warn the superintendent to make all arrangements strictly on the Q.T.'

'I'll take care of that.'

'Well, now – I think – we've fairly staged the scene for Holtsner's final appearance, so it only remains for you to ring up the Blankborough superintendent – the curtain must wait till tonight – while I go and secure a car.'

'What time do you propose starting from town?'

'We don't want to reach our destination before dusk, so if we leave about seven-thirty, that will get us to our rendezvous by nine o'clock.'

'Then I had better mention that to the superintendent when phoning?'

'Of course. Tell him nine or thereabouts; better make it rather before than after.'

'Where shall we meet, sir?'

'Oh, at my flat in Whitehall Court – you know the number. Come early and we'll have a bite of something before starting.'

'Thanks, I'm much obliged.'

'So long then, Brown – don't forget your warrant for arrest.'

Shortly after dusk four men silently approached the garden door of Holtsner's museum: Rhymer, Brown, and two stalwart fellows from the local police force; the latter having met the car, containing the former, at a prearranged spot on the outskirts of the town.

'Conceal yourself with the two men behind that bush, Brown, while I manoeuvre the enemy's camp,' Rhymer enjoined as he crept up to the door. He found it shut. Bending down he peered through the keyhole. The inspection appeared to satisfy him, for he turned and beckoned to the others. They all three approached, led by Brown, and assembled in a group at the threshold. Rhymer then inserted a skeleton key in the latch. Cautiously opening the door he peeped within, and, pointing to the curtained recess, said:

'Inspector Brown and I will hide in there, and you two will return to your former place of concealment. Take this,' he added, giving the foremost of the two the skeleton key, 'but don't attempt to use it under any circumstances, unless you hear two loud blasts of a whistle. Then enter sharp – understand?'

'Yes, sir.'

'Remember not to stir before the given signal.'

The two men saluted and returned to their allotted post, whereupon Rhymer immediately entered the museum with the detective, noiselessly latching the door behind them.

'Now then, quick!' he exclaimed, slipping across the apartment and raising the curtain which covered the recess. A moment later they were both hidden behind its folds.

They were only there about ten minutes – which seemed to them as many hours – when the door communicating with the house suddenly opened. Glancing through a couple of slits in the curtain, they distinguished, in the dim light, Holtsner and his servant Ball entering the room. The former switched on the light, and together they approached the large case with the glass doors. Opening this they lifted out one of the mummy cases, which Rhymer observed was not the same as that they had replaced the night before.

'It's number three's turn now,' Ball remarked with a malicious grin.

Holtsner grunted some unintelligible reply. Then they propped up the box on end against the wall. Holtsner produced a key and unlocking the receptacle of death, threw back the lid, exposing the effigy within.

A gaunt, shrivelled, parchment-like freak was exhibited. The emaciated neck and head surmounted by a shock of tousled hair. The bulbous, moist-lipped mouth leering with vapid expression. Then Holtsner, with a deep sigh, stretched himself upon the couch, while Ball, crouching over him, passed his hands backwards and forwards across the recumbent man's face.

He had not made more than a dozen 'passes' before his body became perfectly rigid, and at the same moment Rhymer observed a distinct tremor passing through the mummified figure occupying the open case.

The Thing appeared to be suscipient to some mysterious endowment of life and motion. Brown evidently observed this manifestation as well, for he laid a trembling hand upon Rhymer's arm, as if to draw his attention to the abnormal change. The Creature's lips were now puckered with a sucking motion, relaxing into a diabolical grin. Then the nostrils dilated, as though about to renew their former function of breathing – and – then – two shrill screams pierced the horrible silence. Rhymer could stand it no longer. He had seen enough.

'Brown,' he cried as he replaced the police whistle in his pocket, 'get your pistol ready,' and smartly drawing back the curtain, the rings rattling along the rod supporting it, discovered himself and his companion to the other occupants of the room.

The effect of this dramatic stroke was instantaneous, for Holtsner immediately awoke, and leapt off the couch. Simultaneously the flicker of returning animation left the mummified corpse, while Ball and Holtsner – their features distorted with uncontrollable fury – sprang, with one accord, towards the intruders.

Their action, however, was abruptly checked by the gleaming barrels of their adversaries' pistols. Then the sound of a key grating in the latch of the garden door caused the two Boches to wheel round in that direction, only to find their retreat cut off by the entry of two more men similarly armed.

'Hands up! Herr Graf Friedrich von Verheim and Otto Krupp of the German Secret Service,' cried Rhymer, 'attempt any resistance and you'll be shot at sight as dangerous spies. The game's up, let me tell you.'

The two men instantly obeyed, unadulterated 'Hate' written broadcast on their faces. Turning to Brown, Rhymer added:

'Search these men for any weapons they may have concealed.'

The subsequent examination only produced a sheathed knife, found on the pseudo Alfred Ball.

'What's the meaning of this unwarrantable outrage?' Von Verheim blustered with a forced expression of outraged innocence. '*Himmel!* but I'll have the law upon you for forcing your way into my house.'

'It's no use, Von Verheim, we've nabbed you red-handed, and Detective-Inspector Brown, here, from Scotland Yard, has a warrant for your arrest, so you'd better come quietly.'

'Bah! What evidence have you?' he sneered with a cunning look of effrontery.

'Sufficient to have you both convicted and hanged for conniving in the act of wilful and premeditated murder.'

At this retort a vague look of relief illuminated the crafty face of the Boche.

'So!' he hissed with unbridled derision, 'you think, then, you clever pig of an Englishman, that one of your juries will convict me and my comrade of murder, committed by some madman running riot about the country, and whom your clever policemen are incapable of arresting.'

'No, Von Verheim, it won't be necessary for a jury to convict on that score, for we've a far graver charge to bring against you and your accomplices than murder – in the ordinary sense of the word.'

Von Verheim arrogantly raised his eyebrows.

'The contents of a notebook in your safe over there—'

'*Mein Gott!*' he gasped, interrupting Rhymer as the latter produced this trump card. His face underwent an appalling change. From a semblance of arrogance and bravado, it assumed a deathly pallor. '*Ach Himmel!*' he spluttered. 'So! you've been to that safe – Otto, what did I tell you? I suspected these English pigs were thieves. *Donner und blitzen!* What will the All Highest say?'

Then, in a burst of frenzy, turning his twitching face towards his confederate, he cried:

'The elixir – quick, Otto – I'm faint – the bottle – it's in the drawer there!'

The servant made a move in obedience to Von Verheim's demand, but was quickly arrested in the act by a sharp command from Rhymer:

'Move another step,' he cried, 'and you're a dead man. I'll get the bottle.' And, motioning Brown to keep an extra watchful eye on Otto Krupp, he quickly approached the table indicated by Von Verheim. The latter made a sly movement as though to intercept him, but was promptly pulled up by the detective.

'Remember you're covered by the police officers behind you,' he barked, 'and they've instructions to shoot.'

The threat was effectual, and Rhymer reached the table without further interruption. Opening the drawer, he produced a small though businesslike bomb, quite big enough to have blown the whole place to atoms.

'So this is your bottle of elixir, Von Verheim?' he queried with sarcasm, regarding the Boche with a gleam of triumph in his eyes. 'An effective dose, too, for strafing the safe and its contents, ourselves into the bargain. I suppose that wouldn't have been of any account, provided you were able to obliterate all evidence of your Hunnish plot.'

Without giving Von Verheim the opportunity of replying to this indictment, Rhymer nodded to the officers behind, who prompdy seized both the Boches and handcuffed them.

So expeditiously was this accomplished that the prisoners were afforded little, if any, opportunity of resistance.

'Now,' he exclaimed, 'Inspector Brown will read the warrant.'

While this formality was being discharged, Von Verheim and his accomplice maintained a forced attitude of indifference, and not until the two officers began to lead them away, did either of them evince any further sign of protest. Then, with a look of malignant 'Hate', Von Verheim, turning towards Rhymer, shouted:

'I hate your country! I loathe your government! Let them murder me and my comrade. What do we care? Bah! We defy you, even now. Kill the body – yes – and you release the spirit to live and effect a greater vengeance – inflamed by the unquenchable fire of eternal "Hate".'

A casual observer might have construed this furious tirade as nothing more or less than an outburst of rage proceeding from a man baffled in the pursuit of a long-prepared scheme of revenge. But to Rhymer it conveyed an extremely subtle threat, beneath which lurked an element of significance, far deeper than anger alone could account for. However, he made no comment, beyond a significant motion of his head directing the instant removal of the prisoners, which was promptly effected through the garden door.

Then turning to Brown he abruptly exclaimed:

'We mustn't lose a minute, for there's no knowing who may be lurking about this place, though I believe we have taken these spies completely by surprise. Lock both doors, please, and be ready for any emergency.'

Brown did as he was requested, after which Rhymer opened the safe again with his skeleton key, and securing the notebook, placed it in his pocket.

'Now,' said he, 'as soon as we get back to our hotel, I'll

acquaint you with all the facts I've collected during the last few days. But, before we leave this unhallowed spot, I want to search for another piece of evidence.'

He approached the open mummy case, where it stood propped up against the wall, closely examining the gaping mouth with its row of discoloured teeth. A few seconds later he turned to the inspector, his eyes sparkling with satisfaction.

'Have you got that little box,' he cried, 'you showed me at our first meeting?'

'Yes.'

'Let me have it, then – quick!'

He almost snatched the box from Brown's hand as he produced it from his pocket, and opening the lid took out a tiny piece of some discoloured-looking substance, pointed at one end, carefully placing it between the leering lips of the mummy.

'The exact counterpart!' he cried, a moment later, in a tone of triumph. 'Look, Brown, don't you see what it is?'

'Well, I thought it was a piece of bone,' he ventured with indecision, 'which the surgeon took from one of the victims' necks.'

'Of course it's a piece of bone, or rather ivory, and what's of more consequence still – a piece of one of the *canine* or eye-teeth of this preserved corpse. Don't you see it fits the broken stump, and must have previously been snapped off? It's a BROKEN FANG! Doesn't that suggest a clue?'

'Great Scot, sir! Why, the brute must have bitten that poor fellow, and broken off one of its teeth in the effort! Good heavens! Surely the Thing's not a vampire?'

'That's what I've suspected it to be all along.'

'But I always regarded vampires to be purely mythical,' said Brown.

'When you become acquainted with the contents of this book,' patting the incriminating article in his breast-pocket, 'you'll alter your opinion. However, let me point out something else relating to this Thing here. Look at the skull. Do you see those two small holes?'

Brown signified assent.

'Well, you can't deny that they are bullet holes; therefore the natural inference is that this nondescript Creature met its death, originally, by shooting, which summarily rejects Von Verheim's assertion that it is the corpse of an ancient Egyptian. Firearms weren't used in those remote times.'

'But don't you remember,' Brown hazarded, 'shooting at the Creature in the lane – mightn't that account for the bullet holes in the skull?'

Rhymer regarded the detective for a moment with a half-suppressed look of amusement.

'By Jove, Brown,' he cried, 'you're waking up at last to the psychological probabilities of the case,' and slapping him on the shoulder, added:

'So now you begin to realize that this corpse, like the other we saw, is not quite so defunct as normal conditions would infer. But don't be too cock-sure yet. You've fallen into one error, for I told you I shot that other 'freak' *through the body*, and there is no corresponding bullet mark in the abdominal region of this corpse.'

Brown scratched his head in evident perplexity, then, with a bantering smile, observed:

'When I passed a remark in front of Von Verheim, the other morning, upon the apparently well-preserved condition of these mummies, you promptly shut me up.'

'I admit the charge,' Rhymer responded, 'but I had a good reason for doing so, as you will soon realize. But come,' he continued, 'let's examine a few more of these grotesque coffins before we make tracks.'

Two or three were accordingly wrenched open (they were all fitted with modern locks) and their occupants exposed. An exceptionally hideous specimen was eventually uncovered, which, upon closer inspection, revealed a small hole in the abdomen, with a corresponding bullet flattened firmly against the spinal column behind.

'Now, Brown, what do you think of that? Seems as though more than one agent was employed in these crimes, eh?'

'Looks uncommonly like it.'

'Holloa! What's that?' Rhymer suddenly exclaimed, as his keen glance happened to fall upon a long, dark cloak suspended from a peg in the corner. With a few strides he reached it, and taking it down examined the garment. A moment later his hand was in his pocket, and out came a letter-case, from which he produced a small piece of cloth, and comparing it with the cloak, exclaimed:

'Here you are, Brown, another piece of evidence.'

'What's that?' the inspector enquired as he crossed over to where Rhymer was standing.

The latter, by way of reply, spread out the cloak, exhibiting a gap in the hem from which a piece of the material had been torn.

'See that?' he enquired.

'By Jove! Yes, and you've got the missing fragment?'

Rhymer triumphantly waved aloft a small piece of frayed cloth, exclaiming:

'This is the identical piece I found in my hand after my "scrap" the other night with the vampire.'

'And it matches the ulster.'

'Perfectly.'

'Well, I'm—'

'No, you're not yet,' Rhymer hastily interrupted, 'but let's get out of this, or there's no saying what might happen. It's a confoundedly rum spot,' and buttoning up his coat, he switched off the light, and followed by the inspector, made his exit through the garden door.

'It is quite evident,' said Rhymer in the course of a conversation with the detective later the same night, 'that any one who investigates the phenomena of psychology, will, at some time or other, come across complicated influences devoid of explanation by common or garden theories. Now the case we have in hand seems to be one of these. Of course you've heard of the widespread and ancient belief in vampires – bodies which the earth has rejected, and, therefore, do not properly decay?'

'Yes, but as I recently remarked, I only regarded them as fairy tales.'

'Well, as I said before, I think you'll alter your opinion, if you haven't done so already, when you've heard all I have to tell you. To begin with, vampires are accredited with sucking the life-blood from their victims, and, as you have already told me, the police-surgeon attributed the death of the Blankborough victims as primarily due to some bloodsucking process—'

'Yes, by Jove! But you'd never get a judge and jury to accept such a theory, let alone convict on it.'

'I've no intention of asking for a conviction on that count; but do let me get on with what I have to say. This manuscript contains sufficient evidence to convict both our prisoners as dangerous spies, without introducing these murders or any psychical proof at all. Von Verheim is a distinguished German scientist and psychologist, so I fished out when in London, whose decease was falsely reported many years ago, and who has been residing in this country all the time, unsuspected.'

'Then he was naturalized under the name of Holtsner.'

'Naturally, and being employed by the German Secret Service, was supported by them in his deception.'

'That shows the war has long been contemplated by the Huns,' said Brown.

'There's no doubt about that. But, confound it all, what a chap you are to interrupt. Well, so much for Von Verheim, and now we come to Otto Krupp. He was an old pupil of the former, and a qualified chemist. A shrewd fellow, too, who has obtained a complete mastery of the English language—'

'That's very evident,' said Brown, 'for he took us both in, pretty neatly, at the King's Arms the other evening, with his Cockney speech and accent.'

Rhymer, ignoring the interruption, continued:

'There is a very brief but sufficiently clear record in Von Verheim's notebook, of a monstrous scheme for the importation over here of the corpses of German soldiers killed in battle: these bodies having previously been immersed in some special preparation – discovered by him – for definitely arresting decomposition—'

'Now I see why you wanted the chief to have all cargoes examined, coming through neutral ports.'

'Exactly, for these bodies were to be sent over, camouflaged as Egyptian mummies, and delivered at the private residences of various naturalized Germans. These wretched aliens are described by Von Verheim as "mediumistic" and capable of freeing, at will, the spirits from their bodies, and then, by "possessing" these preserved corpses, convert them into vampires, "controlling" them to commit any atrocities their Teutonic imaginations might devise.'

'Then that's what Von Verheim was up to in the museum when we interrupted him.'

'Undoubtedly, and by means of this demoniacal agency, they hoped to commit wholesale murders with little chance of discovery.'

'What on earth did they hope to achieve by such a course?'

'An expansion of the Boche mania for "frightfulness", I imagine; although the written evidence reveals that only fit men of military age were to be attacked by these vampires. This looks as though they were plotting to diminish the strength of our fighting units as well.'

'Then the mutilating business was evidently a cunning attempt to conceal the vampire element?'

'Exactly.'

'The whole thing seems too horrible,' Brown exclaimed, aghast, 'it's barely credible.'

'I repeat, nothing is incredible where the Boche is concerned; we've already had sufficient proof of that.'

'I wonder why Krupp made that convicting admission about the missing knife at the King's Arms the other night?'

'Presumably with the hope that some one might have chanced to pick it up, and overhearing to whom it belonged, would promptly return it to him or his master.'

'He little thought that it would lead to their ultimate detection.'

'No; but they were on the alert. The figure you followed last night hadn't a knife, so they evidently abandoned the mutilating "stunt" as too risky. I've also ascertained that the fourth victim, murdered last night, was not mutilated.'

'But do you believe this scheme could have been extensively worked?'

'Most decidedly. The assassinations would have spread broadcast, and these vampires, whose strength – when possessed with temporary life – is prodigious, would have played the very deuce, if once the evil had got a firm hold.

For though the Boche has yet to be born whom any average Britisher would fear to tackle, and knock out into the bargain, still, there is a limit to all human endurance: and even the bravest amongst us would look askance when faced with a supernatural menace like this.'

'That I readily admit.'

'Exactly. Well, vampires are invulnerable, and unless unearthed and literally dismembered or burnt, when in a condition of inactivity, they cannot be suppressed. So the only effective remedy for the evil is that which we are adopting, in discovering the whereabouts of the living fiends who are "possessing" these vampire bodies, and forcibly removing them out of harm's way.'

'It'll be a difficult job to find the others,' said Brown.

'I think not, for Von Verheim was the head and moving spirit in the entire scheme, and by now he and his accomplice will be safely under lock and key. The notebook, remember, contains a list of those aliens over here concerned in the conspiracy, as well as an entry of the four Blankborough victims – we saw Von Verheim enter the last – which I shall send to your chief. In addition, documentary evidence here proves that Von Verheim and Krupp have been involved in conveying important information to the enemy, which has been puzzling the authorities for some time past. This evidence, alone, is sufficient to convict them. However, unless I'm much mistaken in your chief, the remainder of the gang will soon be interned or even more efficiently disposed of.'

'It's a good job I sought your assistance when I did, sir,' Brown exclaimed with an expressive nod of his head, 'for though we shan't be able to satisfy the public as to who the perpetrators of these atrocities are, we have, undoubtedly, knocked on the head a very grave menace to the country. A great pity the B.P. won't know this, since they'll be sure to blame us police for apparently failing to bring home these crimes to the real culprits.'

'Never mind,' said Rhymer, 'console your official mind with the knowledge that you, your chief, and I have learned the truth, and we shall shortly get our own back in the satisfaction of knowing that Von Verheim and his gang have got their deserts.'

'After all, that's some recompense,' Brown admitted – still hankering after public recognition.

'Some? – A great deal, I call it, since a widespread catastrophe has narrowly been averted. And our job, after all, is to serve King and Country, and if we've done that to the best of our ability, "then," say I, "hang public opinion." '